To all the children who need a parent's love tonight. I pray you find it soon. – APGE

To Kenny, Amy, and Adam for all your love and support. – HBMC

Thanks to Mary, Matthew, and staff at City of Glasgow College

Alex's mom and dad sat down on his bed and said,

"We're going to be a foster family."

Alex's nose scrunched up, his chin went down, and his eyebrows met together in the middle.

"What's a foster family?"

"It means I'm putting together your old crib," Dad said.

"It means more kids to play with," Mom said.

The following week, the doorbell rang. A lady with a huge stack of papers held a small boy.

"Look," Alex's mom said. "This is Malik, your new foster brother."

"Twuck, big truck," Malik said and ran towards Alex's fire truck.

Alex's nose scrunched up, his chin went down, and his eyebrows met together in the middle.

"No! No playing with my fire truck, or my superhero, and especially not my bike."

Malik was a *lot* of trouble.

At breakfast, Malik ate *Alex's* chocolate corn flakes. At naptime, Malik stole *Alex's* elephant.

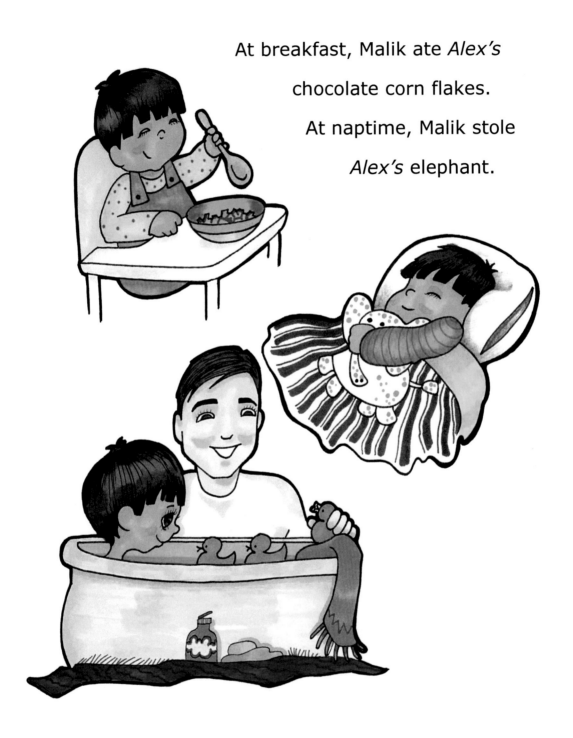

And at bath time, Dad played rubber ducks with *Malik*.

The next day, after lunch, Malik cried.

"Mama, Mama."

Alex's nose scrunched up, his chin went down,
and his eyebrows met together in the middle.

"Sure, have her." Alex pushed Malik towards his mom.

"No. Mama. Mama!" Malik said and ran away.

"He wants his tummy mommy," Alex's mom said.

"I'm Malik's foster mom, but he has a mom who carried him in her tummy."

"Just like I came out of your tummy?" Alex asked.

"Yes," Alex's mom said. "He misses her."

"Oh." Alex walked over to Malik.

"You can play with my trains. They'll make you happy."

Malik smiled.

He was kind of cute for a baby brother.

The next couple of months, Malik and Alex had lots of fun.

They built tall skyscrapers.

They splashed in mud puddles.

And they helped Dad build the best playground ever.

Then the lady with so many papers came back.

"Malik has to leave," Dad said.

"He's going back to his tummy mommy," Mom said.

"No," Alex shouted.

"No," Malik yelled.

"Woof-woof," the dog barked.

"I'll give Malik my fire truck and my superhero man
if he can stay," Alex said.

"No," said Alex's mom.

"His tummy mommy is going to do lots of fun things with him. He'll be happy at home."

Alex's nose scrunched up, his chin went down, and his eyebrows met together in the middle.

But the lady with all the papers picked up Malik and left.

Alex's dad pulled him up on his lap.

"Remember when your friend Conner came over to
spend the night?
You had so much fun. But in the
morning, Conner had to go back to his home."

Alex tried not to sniffle.
"And Malik has to go to his home?"

"Yes," Dad said.

Alex missed Malik.

But Alex had lots of fun with his mom and dad.

They rode a roller coaster.

They went boating on a lake.

And they saw dinosaurs at a museum.

One day, the lady with the paperwork rang the doorbell again.

She held a tiny baby.

"This is Bonnie," Mom said. "She's your foster sister."

"Maybe she would like to see my fire truck,"
Alex said.

"Maybe," Mom said.

"Will Bonnie have to leave someday like Malik?"

"I don't know," Mom said. "It depends if her tummy mommy gets all better or not."

"Will I have to leave someday too?" Alex asked.

"No," Alex's mom said. "I'm your forever mom."

Alex smiled. "Good. Maybe if Baby Bonnie can't go back to her tummy mommy, you can be Bonnie's forever mom too."

Alex's mom smiled. "Maybe."

53698399R00020

Made in the USA
San Bernardino, CA
16 September 2019